Betty & James
The love triangle

Kathryn_Folklore

Ukiyoto Publishing

All global publishing rights are held by

Ukiyoto Publishing

Published in 2022

Content Copyright © Kathryn_Folklore

ISBN 9789360167639

All rights reserved.

No part of this publication may be reproduced, transmitted, or stored in a retrieval system, in any form by any means, electronic, mechanical, photocopying, recording or otherwise, without the prior permission of the publisher.

The moral rights of the author have been asserted.

This is a work of fiction. Names, characters, businesses, places, events, locales, and incidents are either the products of the author's imagination or used in a fictitious manner. Any resemblance to actual persons, living or dead, or actual events is purely coincidental.

This book is sold subject to the condition that it shall not by way of trade or otherwise, be lent, resold, hired out or otherwise circulated, without the publisher's prior consent, in any form of binding or cover other than that in which it is published.

ACKNOWLEDGEMENT:

Noel M. Alvarez

Helen F. Alvarez

Norvin John F. Alvarez

Samantha Festin

Kaitlyn Festin

Anthony James F. Libiran

Sheena Libiran

Maria Ysabelle Garcia

Apple Rural

Vianne Catudio

Angela Mardo

Chelsey Domingo

Gabrielle Base

KC Hernandez

Eunice Charmagne Varon

Karla Sebastian

Dedication

Dedicated to Taylor Swift, My family, my Friends and especially, you; the Readers

Contents

Cardigan	1
The One	5
The Lakes	10
Mirrorball	15
Betty	21
August	24
James	30
This Is Me Trying	34
Invisible String	39
Seven	45
Illicit Affairs	51
Hoax	56
Tears Ricochet	61
Mad Woman	67
The Last American Dynasty	72
Exile	78
Peace	84
About the Author	*86*

Cardigan

I think I'm in love with James. It all started when he approached me in the homeroom. It was a few months ago. We were seatmates. He usually is a shy guy. He shared some funny or cute quotes and notes when it was homeroom time.

I thought I saw James at the bus stop. He wasn't there. I remember him when he always nervously smiles at me and then says 'Hey Betty'. His eyes showed me how genuine he was. How he only talks to me and told me he hates the crowds. His sweet disposition and wide-eyed gaze. Something that always felt at home in my heart. I walked inside the school corridors. It was my favorite class followed by breaks and lunchtime: Homeroom. It's where I get to hang out with James most of the time. We have been together for about 3 months now.

I entered the room where the teacher was not yet around. Turned on the lights myself, and I was early. I always attend class at 7:30 am. Inez came in gossiping with her friends. They were laughing. I just don't know why they always spread rumors.

James wasn't around yet. His vacant chair and desk made me hope he wouldn't be late. Inez walked closer to me. She approached me on her cell phone.

"Hey, Betty. Can I talk to you about James?"

She had a concerned look on her face. Why does she want to talk about James anyway? I never believed the things she said. Mostly it consists of gossip that ruins others' reputations.

"I actually saw James's fighting with Dylan." I looked at her with disbelief. I believed James would not harm Dylan. She then showed her phone. But it was a voice recording. It didn't sound like James at all.

"I don't believe you, Inez."

That's all I have said to her. She left disappointed that I didn't believe her. After all, Dylan and I are best friends. He wouldn't harm any of my friends. She always wants to ruin James' reputation since he rejected her.

7:40 am was when James came inside homeroom class. The time when the teacher was almost going to class was 8:00 am. His messy brown curly hair, and his green eyes, had always made me happy. He was carrying a red-wrapped gift box. A gift that he gave to me later after he sat beside me.

"How sweet of you James." I then took out my notebook and pen so I could get ready for homeroom. He had given me a photo album with polaroid pictures that contained our pictures from our trip together had all the other sweet moments together. Along with a white cardigan that was my favorite gift from him.

"Did you fight with Dylan?" He then smiled and assured me that he would never do that. He then told me that Dylan and he are friends. I began to think there was no problem at all between them.

"I believe you; Inez told me earlier that you fought with my best friend. That cannot be true of course, she had a fake recording that she made on her phone."

He then kissed my cheek. He whispered his promise that he would never hurt anyone that I am friends with or try to even hurt me.

The teacher came and we began our attendance checking. Our teacher had round glasses, he wore a vest and he dressed like a smart person. When he was done we were told to give two classmates an apology or thank you letter.

James and I began writing thank you letters to each other. I wrote my letters in a notebook. Wearing two pages after I was done. I even wrote a letter to Inez to stop gossiping about rumors. I gave the two letters to whom I wrote.

The homeroom class ended.
So we went to the next class.
The rest of the day was great.
I spent time with James after school.
And we both enjoyed listening to Taylor Swift's music

on my phone, enjoyed sharing popcorn, and watching movies we picked at the cinema.

James began to talk to me about how he plans to be my dance partner at prom tomorrow. He was smiling at me. It was all like a dream that day. It was peaceful, full of sweet memories.

[1]Author's NOTE!!

This is based on Taylor Swift's songs of folklore not just about Betty. It was before the narrative of the song. **James and Betty have been dating for almost a year.**

---

[1] This is based on Taylor Swift's songs of folklore not just about Betty. It was before the narrative of the song happened. I am making it into a slower pace that is not yet in the song... This is the chapter where I just introduced Betty first. Cardigan is a perfect song for it. James wasn't talking much here since I will include it in a different chapter. I picked a cardigan for the first chapter since it suits it better. The most relevant chapter will be separated chapters of Betty and James' Point of view of the song Betty

The One

August's Point of view.

I joined the cheerleading squad. It was the best decision for me since I could become a scholar. My name is August Summers. My parents named me August since I was born that month. I have a problem with my family. Financially, we are stable. But my parents fought last night, I don't have a brother or sister to hang out with.

Things get harder by myself. I was wondering why my past relationships never last. It was a fast-paced relationship with about 3 boyfriends, and all of them did something wrong to me. I'm still a virgin as far as I can remember.

My ginger brown hair was tied into a messy bun, my blue eyes were closed as soon as I was thinking about what happened yesterday night. Things got tight in my family budget.

I went to the cheerleading squad. Saw my ex-boyfriend Ashton kissing the gossip girl of the school here in the hallway in front of the janitor's closet. A good hiding place where the CCTV cameras can't see them. I don't know her that much, all I know is her name. But things got a little tough between me and

Ashton. All I wanted was to move on, a peaceful mind without thinking of boys.

I do not need a rebound boy, I got my friends with me... Single people still can have fun. It wasn't as bad as breaking up with someone. It hurts when someone like Ash could treat me with silence when he met that girl when we were together. Inez then pulled away from the kiss and cuddled. She looked at me and said, batting her eyes:

"Hi there, Summer you seem to be a bummer." She laughed at herself. I passed by her walking away since the class was about to start. I am okay with this today, ignoring her felt good.

As I was carrying my books and heading toward the class. I arrived on time and the teacher was sitting down in his seat. His eyes were engrossed in his attendance sheet. My best friend Katie was sitting beside the seat I had. We were classmates and seatmates. How lucky I am to be close to such a caring person. She smiled at me patting the seat beside her. Gesturing for me to sit down quickly. "Ms. Summers, are you present?" Mr. Andrew Santos our Filipino teacher said. It was a language class so it was natural if we learn that language. It was a bit hard for me to pronounce the words. Living in the United States can be very diverse.

"Yes, I am present Sir Andrew."

I glanced as if someone was whispering my name. I turned my back to see Ashton. He was newly assigned here in this class. He then gave me a note. I wonder if he would just mind his own business.

I looked at the note. It says:

I know I have done you wrong. I lost feelings for you. I am sorry that Inez called you a bummer. She just made it rhyme. I began to love her even though we were in a relationship. Can we still be friends Sam?"

He usually calls me 'Sam' mixing the alphabet of the names August and Summer and shortening it. I then gave him back the note and just said "no".

He then nodded that he understood me. I turned around to listen to the class. Now discussing nouns in Filipino.

"Pa-nga-lan," The teacher began and we repeated what he said. "Please turn your modules to page 35. Bring out your books please." He instructed. He fixed his glasses making them closer to his eyes. He had this Asian accent that is kind of funny. I began to think about how learning languages is actually like starting Grade 1 in a different country. We then bring out our books. Katie then whispered to me asking what page it was. "Thirty-Five, Katie." We then continued the lessons.

Betty was here in class. That new girl that most guys in the class wanted to date. She was beautiful yet she lacked confidence. She always hangs out with this guy called James. I don't know if she is dating at all. They don't kiss in public or hold hands. Maybe I just don't know. I kind of liked James. He isn't a playboy like my past exes. Now I think I shouldn't be friends with him. Betty might think I am going to get him from her.

After the class, we had planned to audition for the cheerleading squad. Katie and I have been excited about the cheerleading session. Because finally, I joined in the middle of the year. She is a sporty girl but she decided cheerleading was fun. She joined earlier than me. We began eating our food. We had apples, apple juice, bacon and mac and cheese, and fries on top of a white plate and blue tray. Lunch was delish, even though I was on a diet. I started talking to Katie about my problems and the reason why I joined cheerleading late.

"You know that the other girls in school would want to join like you. I am the cheerleading captain so I am allowed to let you join since you passed the tryouts." The way she said it was sweet which made me smile. I thanked her, then I ate my mac & cheese finishing it until taking my last bite of it. Katie had brown hair, wore glasses, and had a fair complexion.

Then James approached our table.
"Why do you want to talk to me?"
He smiled at me with a reply that made me feel good.

"I wanted to be friends with you. I think Inez is up to something. I'm tired of her rumors and lies. I know your ex-boyfriend is Ashton. Just wanted you to talk to me. We aren't that close but we both don't like Inez."

His eyes were troubled. He wasn't okay. Is there something wrong with him and Betty?

The Lakes

James' Point of view.

Betty did not notice me at the bus stop. She glanced but did not say anything. I entered the bus and I saw that she was the last to go inside. I was there in the back seat wearing my hoodie jacket, vintage tees, Levi jeans, and Vans sneakers.

I went a bit late to homeroom. I was so happy to see her. Not everybody knew about our official relationship.

When I entered the classroom. I approached the vacant seat beside Betty. Gave her a gift when I sat down and talked to her. She opened the box and saw the white cardigan I gave to her. She loved to have a cardigan so I decided to give it to her. She then saw the album of our polaroid pictures of moments we shared.

"How sweet of you James,"

She said placing my gift in her backpack. She then looked at me with eyes that were concerned about what was happening to me.

"Did you fight Dylan?" I then looked at her, in shock. I began thinking of how Dylan wanted her. But of course, I was the one who got to be her boyfriend.

"Why would I do that? Dylan and I are on good terms. I am sure that I did not fight with him. I and Dylan are friends since he is your best friend, Betty. Why did you ask? Is everything alright?"

She then smiled at me and answered: "I believe you, Inez told me earlier that you fought with my best friend. That cannot be true of course, she had a fake recording that she made on her phone." Then I kissed her on the cheek. She is so cute when she believes me.

"I would never do anything to hurt you, Betty, I promise."

I whispered promising her those things would never happen. The teacher came inside. We greeted him and proceeded with the attendance recording. She then exchanged short post-it notes with me. As the day continued I was bothered by thoughts on Inez's rumors.

I went to find a girl who also had problems with Inez. I heard of one girl. Her name is? It's August Summer. I ate my lunch, which was too plain for me. I looked for August. She was at the usual popular table with her best friend.

"Why do you want to talk to me?"

She asked in a calm voice. It was my first time talking to her. I admit that she looks beautiful. But I still have a relationship with Betty to consider.

"I wanted to be friends with you. I think Inez is up to something. I'm tired of her rumors and lies. I know your ex-boyfriend is Ashton. He is now Inez's boyfriend. Just wanted you to talk to me. We aren't that close but we both don't like Inez."

I was troubled with thoughts that made her. "You can meet me at the mall this weekend." She replied in an enthusiastic tone.

"Saturday sounds good." I agreed with her. I left her so that she could continue her lunch.

Classes were dismissed early today. I looked for Betty around the school. I saw her in the art room. The art room was filled with student's artwork. Sculptures and a large shelf and drawers for art materials.

Betty was an Artist. In my opinion is the best artist in school. I can barely even draw stick figures correctly. She can paint, sketch, carve sculptures, and do anything related to art. She was sitting in front of a painting covered under a cloth.

"Hi, James! Is this nice? I really wanted to show you this."

She stands up, and removes the cloth, revealing that it was a painting filled with shapes. There is a cube that created an illusion of some sort. Hard to describe for me. I'm not an expert at this. I think it's a form of cubism. "It's a great painting, like a form of cubism. Wanna hang out somewhere?"

She then nodded and kissed me on the cheek. "How about the lakes in Mountain Springs?" She nodded.

"I want to go there today. Come on, Let's go; I will drive us there."

I grinned, and she then giggled excitedly to go there. I had my mp3 in my bag. Which was perfect since I could play music. I was ready to go to the lakes. I had a picnic cloth in my bag. Everything was going perfectly. I also brought popcorn for us to enjoy.

She walked swiftly so that she could get her car from the parking lot.

"James get in!"

She said loudly. I walked fast towards the car parked in front of me. I opened the front door of the car. Sitting beside Betty as she drove us to the lakes. The car was an SUV. It was comfortable for both of us.

We arrived at the lakes. It got a bit dark, so I placed the picnic cloth on the grass near the lake. I do not intend on fishing at the lake. It was a bit cold and dark. I just wanted to relax today with Betty. We sat on the picnic cloth.

I got the mp3 from my bag along with the popcorn. I placed the popcorn on the picnic cloth. Plugged the earphones into the mp3 player.

"James the dance is tomorrow."

She smiled, leaning her head on my shoulder. I was holding her hand as we sat watching the stars. I began setting up the music.

"Can you dance with me tomorrow?" She said yes which made my heart fill with glee. "As long as you are there James." She gets the earphone that has an 'r' on it which indicates it was for the Right ear.

It played a song that was our favorite song. Called Little Things by One Direction. And the other songs were Taylor Swift's Red album songs. We both looked up at the stars. Enjoying our popcorn and the few hours that passed. "I need to get home now-" I then told her that it was fine. I will drive her home.

She helped me pack our things. The stars above us we're beautiful tonight. We both went into the car. I was in the driver's seat and she was beside me. I drove her home.

We arrived at her house. A wooden house with a front porch and deck. I kissed her goodbye not knowing this could be the last time.

Mirrorball

Betty's Point of view

I was at home, the air was fresh, I prepared myself then I went downstairs smelling the breakfast that is now cooking in the kitchen. It is the start of a new day. A new day to dance at the school gym at prom. I ate pancakes with my mother. My mom was smiling at me since I told her that her pancakes tasted good. The kitchen was beside the dining room. It is a beige wooden kitchen with pink granite table tops.

"I am going to prom with James later. I know he doesn't like the crowds but I'm sure he would dance with me tonight." I then looked at the time, it was 9:00 am I'm the morning. My mom then asked me if he would pick me up. I then nodded in response. When we were both done. I went upstairs to get ready.

A pink cocktail gown was placed on my bed. It was pretty, would James like it? I then went into the washroom and prepared myself to be ready for the night. Taking a shower and singing a song that I wrote for James. I smiled at the thought that he would dance with me later. The feeling was great, I hoped he would be there with me.

When I was done, I wore my bathrobe, my hair covered by a towel. I looked at the bathroom mirror wondering what kind of makeup I would be wearing after dinner. I was excited about this event and eventually wore my slippers before going out of the bathroom. Time for glow-up time!

James' point of view.

I remembered how I and Betty kissed. It was the best kiss I got from her, when I left her, I remember how August looked at me in the cafeteria. Why am I having mixed feelings for both of them?

Yeah sure, August has a charm that makes me want to get to know her. Things felt worse when I realized that I will meet August at the mall tomorrow. I feel bad that I was thinking about August. I then looked around my room. Things weren't organized like they used to be. My father knocked on my bedroom door.

"You better get ready, It's afternoon right now." He said and went downstairs. I began fixing my hair and doing what a normal human being does during the morning. I went downstairs and saw Dad who was eating lunch, mom wasn't here at home yet. Dad was usually working from home. I always saw my Dad more than my mother. My mom was already gone to work. I ate with my dad in silence and we only heard each other chewing our food.

When I was done, I remembered today is when prom was going to start. I had almost forgotten that I will pick up Betty later. I stood up to place my plate and fork and spoon at the kitchen sink, started cleaning my dish.

My Dad asked me to wash his dishes also. I then started scrubbing the dishes with a sponge. I finished doing the dishes and then placed them into the dish storage for them to dry up. I washed my hands and then walked into the living room. My Dad was watching television for afternoon shows.

"Dad, can I borrow your car tonight? I am going to pick up Betty later this evening." I then saw my dad smiling. "So, prom is tonight right son?" I then nodded, and he smiled. "Just remember to not do anything wrong. I will lend you the car so that you and your girlfriend can enjoy it. Don't avoid the crowds so that you can have a fun son!" He laughed and then gave me the car key.

Later this afternoon, I began preparing myself for the night. I have a bad feeling since crowds are what I consider loud, crowded like a pack of sardines, and I feel nervous when I am with other people besides Betty. After that, I took a bath and brushed my teeth. I wore a white polo shirt, a midnight blue tuxedo, and a black necktie.

I looked at the clock and realized I was going to be late. I realized it took a long time to prepare myself. I had a hard time earlier with the necktie. I ran downstairs in a hurry, I used the car keys to start the car. I arrived late at Betty's house standing on the porch in front of the main door.

Her mom opened the door and frowned. "Why did you keep my daughter waiting? -" A few moments later after she turned her head to see if her daughter was ready. "Betty! Your boyfriend is here!" She called her daughter.

When I saw her coming down the stairs. I was in awe, it was the beautiful dress she wore and her elegance that made me smile. Her hair was curled, her dress was sparkling pink with lace sleeves, and her makeup was simple which enhances her natural beauty. I grinned when I saw her, what a beautiful person she is.

She then walked in front of me and hugged me. She pulled away from her hug then I took a few steps down from the porch approaching my father's car. I opened the front seat door for her. I gave her my hand to guide her to go inside. She gracefully walked into the car removing her hand from mine. I went to the driver's seat, started the car, and drove to school.

When we arrived, I got out of the car so that I could open the door for her. She thanked me and placed her hand around mine. We both gave our tickets to prom. We entered to see the gym decorated in a romantic night theme.

Then I felt like I wanted to go away from such a crowded space. "Is there anything wrong James?" She asked if she noticed that I wasn't feeling great. "Can I just go somewhere else? I am not feeling well right now." She then nodded, and she went to our table. I walked away for a while at the bleachers. I was calming myself down for me to dance later with Betty.

After Betty sat down at her table someone approached her to dance. This song played all of the sudden. I began to quickly walk towards Betty. Just to find out she was dancing with Dylan Blake in front of me. I got jealous so I walked away from her. August approached me and she took my hand and made me follow her.

"James, get in the car." She instructed me. I went in the car... Betty did not notice that I saw her dance with Dylan. I felt cheated. I went inside her car. She then drove to her home. We drank wine which made us drunk. The wine glass and the bottle of wine were placed in the living room. We went upstairs. We slept together which is when I had sex with August. I regretted it. Then Inez, who wasn't supposed to be here at her house saw us together. "What the heck did you both do? I will tell Betty about you both!" She took a picture and left. I was about to stop her but I found out that I was naked. We both realized what we have done. "Why did Inez come inside your house? We didn't even invite her over." I asked August. August told me that Inez has been spying on her and me. We dressed up, and August told me not to worry and that we can both get through the problems that we caused.

Then I wore my clothes and left August. I arrived home. That was when my father asked me where I had gone. "I went to Betty's house." I lied to my dad.

"No, you weren't son ," she called. Betty wants to talk to you on the phone right now."
My dad sounded angry.
Then that was when I found out: Inez told her about me and August.

"Hello...What have you done? Is Inez telling me the truth?"
"Betty...I'm so sorry."
I then heard her crying on the phone.
"Let's break up...I never want to see your face again."

That was the last time Betty talked to me on the phone.

Betty

James was nowhere to be found after he said he would be at the bleachers. I didn't see him when he left me so soon. The bleachers were a bit far to see. I know he hated the crowds so I don't bother to look for him during the Prom dance. Dylan Blake, my best friend, asked me to dance with him. I guess James would mind if I dance with him.

Dylan and I danced the whole night. We even talked about the song that played, and how beautiful the gym was decorated. Then when the prom was nearing its end we both became prom queen and king.

The next morning Inez had texted me. She told me she saw James and August together. She even followed both of them to August's house.

The evidence was that she took a picture of them sleeping together. Both of them were only covered by a blanket, twisted in bedsheets. That was when it all hit hard at me.

James had cheated on me.

Why would he betray me?

I began crying and at first was hesitant to call. I called on his landline, and his dad answered me. "Hello Mr. Reynolds, can I talk to your son? This is Betty speaking." I sighed when he told me that his son wasn't home and he was pretty mad about it.

I then waited in silence. I was heartbroken. My eyes began to fill up with tears. This is the worst thing that ever happened to me.

I then thought that it was the worst thing that ever happened to me to fall in love with James.

I will switch my homeroom soon. I don't want to see his face again.

James called soon after he arrived at his house. "Hello...What have you done? Is Inez telling me the truth?"
I asked him on the phone.

"Betty...I'm so sorry."

Was all he answered.

I started to burst into tears. Crying my heart out before I bring out the courage to break up with him. "Let's break up...I never want to see your face again."

That was the last time James talked to me on the phone.

A few days later I just saw him passed by my house. I felt like I couldn't breathe right now. Part of me still wants him.

The next day I attended a different homeroom class. I was classmates with Ashton and August. I did not hate August for stealing my boyfriend. It was James' fault, not hers.

I wish that James did not lie to me.

But he did.

Now I will host my first party next week.

That party is where everyone would be invited in. I didn't mind if James would come.

I sent out invitations on the next day of school.

Now I wish James go straight to hell.

August

My family's financial problems are going away.
Just like I am leaving this house for tonight.
I got ready for the prom that will take place at the gym.

I cannot stop thinking about him.
His eyes, the way he smiled at me at the cafeteria.
I had a crush on James.

Is this a mistake?

He already has a girlfriend.

It's almost the end of August, the month that I was named.
My birthday was on the 31st of August.

I entered the school gym after I gave my ticket to the event organizer.

The song played was a beautiful song.

I began to look for James.

And I found him.

How does destiny play its game?

It plays it rough.

That's what I thought...

James was near the bleachers while his girlfriend Betty danced with Dylan.

He looked jealous. Maybe I could cheer him up. This is the right moment where would ask him; "James, come with me." I took his hand and made him follow me. I know he had intentions of punching Dylan. It was better that I bring him out of this mess. I said while my heart was racing.

It was like a dream to just hold his hand. I am going to make you mine James. No matter what it takes. He followed me. That was what matters to me now. I wanted to bring him to my house.

I led him toward the school parking lot. I went to my car and opened the door and turned it on using my car key.

"James get in the car."

James went inside my car in the passenger seat beside the driver's seat.

"Where are we going?" I looked at him as he asked me, his eyes staring into mine.

"To my house." I smiled. He nodded, thanking me that he wanted to get out of the gym. He was mad about Dylan dancing with his girlfriend, Betty. I could sense that feeling.

I was always jealous of Betty. Betty has everything while I almost got nothing else but a distant family, a cheerleading squad, and a lonely house. I then focused my eyes on the road.

"We will drink wine and play a game at my house." He then started looking out the window of the car.

"I think that would be fun."

He told me in a non-enthusiastic tone. When we arrived at my house. I opened the main door. I made him wait in the living room. I grabbed some wine from my mother's cabinet. I then went back to the living room.

I then placed the wine on the coffee table. James moved away from the couch he was sitting on and began to sit on the rug. I also sat on the rug right beside him. I turned on the television. It was playing a movie called Me before you.

"Why do you think Betty danced with Dylan?" He grabs a bottle of wine and poured the wine into his wine glass. "Maybe she liked Dylan this whole time," I told him, it made him frown. He gulped the wine as if he was very thirsty. "Maybe you are right." He then looked at the T.V. He pours the wine again and drank it slowly this time.

"That's a sad story... He left her so that he won't be a burden to her as a cripple."

He said he then looked at me. I started to get this feeling... My heart started to pound.

"I think that we should play a game," I told him. He then agreed with me.

"I don't think that we should play any board games. Maybe let's finish all these bottles you brought out. And see who gets drunk first." He told me then I let out a slight laugh.

"Let's go upstairs first," I told him, and he agreed. He was agreeable right at this moment.

We both went upstairs to bring two bottles and one wine glass... I lead him to my room, and placed down the bottles, and a glass that I brought on the floor.

Opened the door and grab the two bottles and the glass carrying it inside my room. He followed... Things got out of hand when we drank all the wine. We both got drunk and we started kissing. He unzipped my cocktail dress. He began to remove his clothes. We had sex on my bed. Twisted in bedsheets. That was it.

I slept beside him. He embraced me and we began to sleep that night.

The next morning... Someone opened the door of my room. It was Inez, I woke up from my sleeping state. Covering myself with my blanket. James also woke up... We were in trouble.

"August what have we done? How did you get here Inez?" James was confused...He just realized that something happened between her and him.

"James? August? What have you both done? Be-Betty would hear about this!"

Inez took a picture. James almost went out of bed. He was naked that's why he didn't stop her.

"How did she get here? Did something happen between both of us?"James asked me. He then quickly got his clothes from the floor.

"I forgot that we left the main door open. Inez might have been spying on us the whole time. We actually did have sex." I told him. He had this regret in his eyes.
We both dressed up. He left me and went home.

I thought I won't hear much from him anymore. He called me and told me that Betty broke up with him. I smiled after the call. Happy that we could be a couple. We began to meet each other at the back of the mall.

A week passed. I canceled my plans for today in case he called.

He never called again.

I went to his house. The salt air and the rust on the doorknob made me feel empty. His Dad answered the door. "Is James around?" I asked his father.

"He is here. James comes down there is a girl over here."
His father said. He came downstairs...He was wearing a white shirt with a cool black design on it.

"Hi, August...So you are attending Betty's party?" He asked me...

That's when I realized he was still in love with Betty.

I was just the girl he had a one-night stand with. He was never really mine after all.

I then nodded and also asked him why he was ignoring me.

I then found out that he was planning on getting back together with Betty.

That was stupid of him...

It was like my world shattered into a pile of puzzle pieces.

James

I am now inside my bedroom. I was in a state of regret at these moments. Good luck with my social problems. Dad is now on the call with the principal. I wasn't able to be punctual like before.

Ever since something happened between me and August. Both of us were having trouble because of how the rumors spread so fast from Inez to the whole school. It was embarrassing and confidential to me. I knew I was wrong about cheating on Betty.

She hasn't returned the things I gave her. She never calls or texts me, she switched classes and became distant. She gained popularity along with Dylan. Dylan wasn't the one who should be her boyfriend. I was supposed to be hers. But it all ended and she started dating him.

Seeing her with him felt bad.

I was sitting down on my bed thinking of what happened in the past few days that turned into a week or more. I then took out her picture with me from my pocket. Wishing her to talk back to me. All that remained was silence and me staring at her smile, the way she used to look at me.

"Betty, I know why you switched your homeroom. It was because of me." I said imagining that Betty could hear me. She ignored me for a week. She wasn't usually like this. I need to make it up to her. I pack my bag to get ready for school. The first hour in class was homeroom. I still can get over the fact that the seat beside me is always vacant!

It really hurts deep in my heart.

The call from Betty sounded which my world shattered into pieces.

It was all my fault. August knew I had a girlfriend at the time.

I only wished I had the power to rewind back time.

But it was all too late.

I know it's my fault to go with August to her house. It was a terrible idea. She shouldn't be involved in this situation. Where did I go wrong? Why had I gained feelings for August in the first place? My blurred memory of that night. The urge to punch Dylan's face. The time when August takes me to her own world of fun, passion, and conversations.

I felt that it was all wrong.
My regret and guilt are eating me up.
I started to lie down on my bed.
Staring at the ceiling of my white bedroom and midnight blue accent walls.

I felt a tear that flowed down to the side of my face. I hate this moment I felt like a cry baby. My dad knocked on the door. "Son... Can we talk?"

He asked me in a kind manner. "Yes, Dad..."

He entered my room and sat down near me while I was lying down on my bed feeling like a hopeless guy who can't make it up to his ex-girlfriend.

"I think the principal called not only because of your punctuality but also you had an illicit affair with a girl. I know you are still young. You may not know anything. You are still my son James. I hope this won't happen again." My Dad said. I was shaking since the principal also was concerned about my personal life.

"I'm sorry Dad. It's just that I get into these moods where I ain't myself." I told him... But part of that wasn't true. I am in fact myself but my mistakes didn't feel like it was me.

If only I had never done what I did to Betty. I Wish I never had an illicit affair with August.

I ask August to hang out with me at the back of the mall.

I thought it could work.

It didn't feel right to me.

A week passed. I forgot to call August. I wasn't in the mood to talk to her.

I never called again. I heard the doorbell when Dad answered the door. "Is James around?" She asked my father. I wished she did not come to my house. All I could think about was Betty and dreamt of her all summer long.

"He is here. James comes down there is a girl over here." I hurried downstairs. Part of me can't decide whether to end my relationship with her or ask her to go to Betty's party with me.

"Hi, August...So you are attending Betty's party?" I asked her politely. She sighed and nodded as her reply. "Yeah, I'm going to her party but...James, why were you avoiding me?" Then a tear fell from her eye like she realized something. "I don't think our relationship will work with August," I told her. The feeling was awkward and sad for both of us. She might be pregnant or not but I do not care about her anymore. All I cared about was making up for Betty.

"I can't be friends with you anymore. Goodbye August."

I closed the door and she whispered her farewell.

This Is Me Trying

Dylan visited me, his eyes seeing me in a different way than before. I ignored James most of the time. I haven't forgiven him yet. I remember the picture Inez sent me. That picture was the only reason why I broke up with him. It caused a pain in my heart that is going to take a long time to heal. I am only thinking of moving on.

From my picture collage with James to the wide range of Taylor swift albums, the teddy bear on my bed that James gave me, and the Cardigan. My favorite Cardigan he gave me during homeroom. All of these are part of my past.

This is me now trying to move on.

I tried to smile, I wished I could just give up the things he gave me. I don't know why I can't. My eyes focused on the cardigan that was hung in my open closet. It was the first thing I wanted to throw away. I just threw it on the floor and it lay under my bed.

Dylan was downstairs. He knew I would get rid of all the gifts James gave me. All I care about now is moving on. I hated that my ex-boyfriend had slept with August.

It hurts me deeply like a knife that slits my wrist. I feel depressed right now. I never wanted to hurt myself because of the mistake he did to me.

I lay down on my bed. Started bursting into tears. Crying my heart out since the breakup a few weeks ago. The truth is all I wanted was for James to still be mine. I respected myself therefore I decided to end things with him. I hated people who aren't loyal, especially when it comes to close relationships.

I had a hard time adjusting to my new homeroom class. Inez wasn't there even James.

Only one face was there.

The girl who had slept with James.

August Summers and I never talked. It was not because I hate her. She was just a reminder of the mistake James made. She tries to approach me sometimes. I just ignored her. Inez became closer to me than before. She would tell me how Ashton had a hard time trusting August for some reason. Ashton had loved August before. It was the same thing that happened to both her and her. Ashton cheated on August. I feel her pain somehow.

How boys treated her like a used doll.

A toy to play with, a blood stain on her dress that never faded.

This is me trying to move on.

Trying to date Dylan helped me cope with all my problems.

All the flashbacks of me and James.

It makes the pain worse than ever.

Dylan knocked on my door. "Betty," I let him in while he kissed my cheek. "Please forget about James. He is such a teenage dirtbag."

"I remember there was a song about that. Called Teenage dirtbag by Wheatus." I then laughed at the thought. His grin was cute, and the corners of his smile showed his dimples. Dylan always likes to mention songs and relate them to people.

"You don't deserve to be treated like an option Betty. You are an amazing person even without James by your side. At least you have me." He sounded genuine about what he said.

Things aren't easy if not many people are by your side. I then remembered that I wanted a party. I will celebrate since I am transferring next year. A party where I can make memories.

The backyard garden was a perfect spot for that party. Everyone already knew about this since I had given invitations. "About the party, can you not invite James?" Dylan asked me then I disagreed.

"I want him to regret what he did to me." Dylan then began to do the secret handshake with me. After that, his arms began to embrace me. I then wrapped my arms around him. "Thank you, Dylan." A tear streamed down my face. This embrace lasted forever in my new memories with Dylan.

He then told me that he can read my diary. "I thought that was personal. Why would you want to read it to me?" He then explained that he wanted me to know how he felt when I was with James.

I then nodded and sat down on my bed. I wanted to know what his story was. He sat beside me and got his small notebook from his pocket. I lay down on his lap and I started to listen to what he would say.

"When you and James met, you were a new girl that guys wanted. James and I both want to get to know you. At first, James was shy, but he wrote you notes and letters during homeroom class. That was when you started liking him.

But me? I started to get to know you by text. Every day we texted. I already knew that James had secured your heart. When I got a chance to be the best friend you wanted. You and James were inseparable. I have had a crush on you ever since.

When I danced with you. I noticed that James was mad and had the urge to punch me. I saw this girl who he had a one-night stand with. She also liked James. And that is how those days are over now. I figured out that James tends to get jealous. Which leads him to lose you and make you one of his options. I think that James had been a bad liar this whole time. Betty, I know me and James had a rivalry. And I wanted to let you know that I love you even if I still remain the best friend you will always have."

"That was sweet." I complimented him. His voice was filled with kindness. I was surprised that Dylan had a crush on me this whole time. "That's why I want you to not give up. Maybe I'm not going to be your last boyfriend. I know that there is always someone who is meant for you."

I wasted all my potential in mourning my broken relationship that can never work out well. "I will leave you for now Betty, I have to go since I have football practice." I then asked him when he will be back. "Maybe Saturday. Bye Betty." He then stood up then left my room.

I don't know if I will allow myself to love Dylan. I feel like I am smart enough to decide on these matters.
If only I would forgive James and let him make it up to me.

This is still me trying to decide.

I think my heart is not ready to break apart again.

Invisible String

James' Dream

"Betty..." He said under his breath. The night when he ultimately failed trying to get back her attention. Deep down in his heart. He knew he messed up.

"Stop it James... I would never forgive you. After what you have done? You are so different from the James I first met."

His wrong actions, all of it was giving him the pain of losing her from his grasps. If only there was a point in asking for forgiveness.

"Betty, I- ca-can explain!" But all Betty did was leave him alone, cutting the connection between both of them.

James woke up, Senior year was a rush to him. He'll wake up and be surprised how much time that has passed by.

The dreams that filled his head were all about fear and an illusion of love that has ended months ago.

Especially, when he kept dreaming of his Ex-girlfriend and the girl, he had a one-night stand with.

The Party

James' point of view

I brought my guitar hoping things would change for the better. But you know what? I've been such a mess. If only she would stop avoiding me. The party that I never got invited to began having more rumors that Betty wants to be popular. But all I know , the guitar, the voice I'll be using to get her to notice me would be enough. Hoping she would accept my apology and I think her party would be worth gate crashing on.

I wasn't the James that she knew.

I wasn't the person to put a smile on her face

anymore.

The burden I brought upon her is all my fault. I lied, cheated and did all the actions she despised in boys. Is singing in her garden worth the try?

For me I would say yes. I'm James after all... Right? For a moment I took a drink from the beer on a nearby counter. Still holding my guitar using my other hand.

I tend to think about the times she deserved someone better than me. Like her boy best friend. For some reason I thought her best friend was gay. Until I saw that they kissed each other last week.

The semester ended after that and a new one started. The last one...

I threw away the empty beer can.

I used my skateboard and started to place my guitar behind my back, wearing it like a back pack.

Apparently, the time I left the house was the time my past regrets started growing within me. Consuming me into an abyss of darkness that made me feel alone.

If only I could mend her broken wings. I would do anything for her just to let her back into my life. It feels awful if I won't be able to take action to correct my wrongdoings.

Dylan saw me arrive at the party. He slowly walked into my direction. He looked mad and acted angry when he saw me.

"Leave Betty alone! Get out of her home, you don't deserve to be hers. Because she has me and you can't do anything about it!"

Dylan pushed me hard and I went out of balance landing on the ground luckily I didn't fell flat on my guitar.

"Dylan, please stop bro. I'm just here to say sorry to her. I can't stop thinking about what I did. I know you want her to be safe. Your her best friend. She probably deserves you, more than I do. All I want is for her to notice me at least I could feel better by then!"

Dylan started to pick me up by my shirt. "Okay, I'll let you apologize. But don't you ever harm her. It's her birthday today and I want you to stop bothering her after that okay? She's mine now."

Dylan then stopped pulling onto the neckline of my shirt. He tried to calm himself down and let me go onto the stage. All of her dumb friends seems to look at me.

Betty went out of her house and into the garden. Her sophisticated black dress made me smile. I then set up my guitar and placed it close to my body.

I memorized the chords of the song that I composed and wrote for her. It will forever remain as the invisible connection between the both of us.

I remember selling yogurt and meeting her there at school and at the shop I'm working at a year ago.

It used to give me enough money to buy my first guitar.

We used to hangout in the School park, having picnics and enjoy conversations. Now the silence became a reminder of how everyone was shocked.

The rumors were true. I started to feel nervous, the first strum of my guitar made me feel relieved.

"Betty, I won't make assumptions
About why you switched your homeroom
But, I think it's 'cause of me
Betty, one time I was riding on my skateboard

When I passed your house
It's like I couldn't breathe."

You heard the rumors from Inez
You can't believe a word she says
Most times, but this time, it was true
The worst thing that I ever did
Was what I did to you
But if I just showed up at your party
Would you have me? Would you want me?
Would you tell me to go fuck myself
Or lead me to the garden?

In the garden, would you trust me
If I told you it was just a summer thing?
I'm only 17, I don't know anything
But I know I miss you
Betty, I know where it all went wrong
Your favorite song was playing
From the far side of the gym
I was nowhere to be found
I hate the crowds,..."

"Shout out to Dylan who've allowed me to sing to you. Betty, please notice me... I know it's my fault and a sorry cannot fix all the wrong things I've done! "

I was expecting Betty to not forgive me after all that happened.

But she approached me and hugged me. Her eyes began to fill up with tears. I didn't know how to react.

I then put back my guitar to the guitar bag and looked at her after singing.

She then dragged me away as I placed my guitar at my back and hand carried my skateboard. She stopped when we were near the gate of her house.

"James... This is enough! There can't be an us anymore. Cheating with August kept me thinking that you are such a jerk! I do forgive you but my heart would never forget what you did. Please leave my house. It is better if we won't be friends at all."

"Fine, I hope you're happy now. Especially with that new boyfriend; Dylan."

Betty then pushed me out of her property.

"Go to hell James!"

This broke my heart. I can't do anything else to make it up to her. Everything feels pointless. Hearing the noises coming from her house made me feel upset that I wasn't part of her life anymore.

She deserves better.

And it's not me.

It doesn't feel right but I'll try my best to be okay.

Seven

"Katie! Run faster!" Katie then started to sprint around the running track at the school gym. Listening and following our coach's commands.

"August...Why are you still here? Is there a problem?" The co-cheer captain asked me. She noticed I was just watching my best friend and the squad doing practice and did not bother to join them.

"Yeah...I don't feel well. I don't think I can practice today or tomorrow. I won't be able to join the squad at the football game."

"More like your pregnant right? Inez might be a gossip girl, but damn! Why would she post about you and James? You don't deserve to be involved in this scandal. The school might even kick the three of you out because of it."

"Don't worry Marzie. I'm not pregnant at all... I just don't know why James ever approached me at the canteen a few months ago. I know maybe it is cuz Inez is a bitch." Marzie tried her best to cheer me up. It wasn't working... She wasn't ready to hear my problem. Nobody ever deserves to know it...

James deserves to...

He just became so unreachable.

Someday, I'll be far away...

Maybe to India?

Somewhere I won't see his stupid face
again!

Maybe I'll change my name...
Those are my thoughts that I kept within my heart.

I'm not sure anymore...
Uncertain about what I should decide for my future.
Everything about him made me feel upset and my self-worth felt horrible right now.
Marzie noticed that I just continued to watch Katie Denver, my only friend who could understand me.

I know James loves Betty...

But I didn't mean to ruin their relationship. Is it really my fault that I have to fix it?

That I longed for James' touch, his eyes to stare into mine... I feel so awful that he can't win Betty back because of what happened between me and James.

And yes, I tried meeting James at the mall. He never came... He never answered my calls anymore. I am disconnected from his life, from his wonderful world that is so out of my league.

"But hey, August! Look, you have to participate in the school work too. Even if your best friend is the cheer captain. You know what I mean... Katie right? The coach tells me that I may be suspended from practice if my grades keep failing. We all can help you. Especially if you need me." While Marzie was telling me this, she tried to wave her hand in front of me to catch my attention.

It wasn't working...

Her help? How can I say to the school that James is going to be?

Wait to stop!
Stop it August!
August and James were never real!

James and Betty were...

And that is my own problem.

Betty was everything he wanted. Of course, it was never me. Never.

He was never mine to love.

My heart started beating fast. Few days after taking the pregnancy test. I felt anxious.

All my what-ifs and loneliness were inside this brain of mine.

I walked away from the practice court. I decided to go to the locker room.

Then I noticed some snoring coming from the janitor's closet. I opened the door. To my surprise it was him.

James was there... He was just sitting on the floor sleeping. He looked restless... as if he was waiting for me.

"James?" I tried to wake him up. Even bothering James' sleep made me feel guilt in my throat. He opened his eyes and saw me.

"August..." He groaned and covered his eyes.

"Why are you here in the closet?"

James begins to look around and see if someone was behind him.

"I was hiding from Betty's new boyfriend. I fell asleep here which was safe enough. August... I don't know what to say to you anymore. I know I hurt you too and it's not all like what Betty felt towards me. Her boyfriend is so protective of her. The world scares me in August. I can't even go to class today and pretend that I attended any classes today." James then covered his eyes. He was fighting his tears.

If only I didn't do it with him at prom night.

"It's okay James... Please forgive me too. I wish I could love you to the moon and Saturn."

I sighed... hoping he will reciprocate all my feelings for me.

But he'd never. His heart was for the popular girl I guess.

"What did you just say to me? I'm nothing. Nothing for you to love. Why pick me when you have a lot of guys crushing on you?"
Why do I ever love him?
Same question as to why this heart always longed for him for many months.
This surprised James for some reason. He was about to open his mouth again to speak.

He didn't respond. I didn't even say anything. We just stared at each other blankly. It was like there was a spark and we couldn't express our feelings to each other.

Minutes later,
he began to smile.
Something came into his mind.

"August, You know what?"

"What?"

"I do, kind of like you..."

"How come?"

"It's just that the day I saw you in the canteen... I wanted to help you. I know your ex-boyfriend went for Inez. And felt that Inez was the one who ruined everything... " He then sighed and took the hat from the shelf and went out of the closet. He then continued his eyes looking into mine.

Just the way I wanted to see it. His eyes, his smile, and everything about him.

"That gossip bitch never stopped talking. You were there... Someone who could help me and I could help you." He then grinned ear to ear. He then moved closer to me and held both of my hands. "We both know Betty was the one I love... Fate cannot change what I feel for her."

What he said broke me. It injured me deeply. Like a knife ran up to my hand and sent shivers down my spine.

I was right he never loved me. But what if I tell him the truth?

"I want you to know about something..."

Then James looked down. Looking at my soft hands that were on top of his.

"What is August? You can tell me that later. Let's meet near the tree and swing close to my house..." He then hurried and left me. I didn't know what to do.

How can I tell him that he'll become a father?

This sucks!

What if he'll keep me waiting?

I can't...

I just can't stop the tears from flowing down my face. The words he told me kept me hurt and unrelieved.

All I thought is that I'll hit my peak at 7. I'll meet him at 7:00 PM.

Illicit Affairs

Jame's point of view

It was 6:00 PM as I was heading home. ***"Make sure nobody sees you leave."*** That was what I always told myself. The candle was lit out of the darkness. The electricity shut down for a while.

I can't figure out another way to make it up to Betty. I did all my alphabetically ordered plans. Her best friend was making sure I felt guilty.

I know damn well that for Betty I'll ruin myself. Everything was falling into place. Betty looked at me at times when I looked and felt horrible.

My body was shaking from the ache after Dylan and his friends made fun of me at school. They even called me a womanizer. All the punches that hit me. Felt good in some way. I deserved it. He and Ashton planned to hurt me. Ashton was mad even if August was already his ex-girlfriend.

He had respect for August. That's understandable. They both fought for the girls they love. And I didn't fight harder for those girls who gave me a feeling of serenity at times like this.

August and Betty. I have mixed feelings about August. Betty gave me a clearer feeling to lose myself from all the doubt I had.

August wasn't part of my future plans. August was my mistake. I was walking in the rain. Hood over my head and kept my head down. I wasn't excited at all to meet August earlier.

She saw me hiding in the closet when I was cutting classes. I knew I'm a good-for-nothing person right now. She gave me hope. I decided to cut off what she was about to say to me.

I was certain that someone else might hear her. I know she'll tell me a secret. Maybe about our first time losing each other's virginity. August was never a whore to me nor a bitch. She was the girl I gave less notice to.

I'm James...
There is Betty who left.
And the new girl I found feels for,

Her name is August.
I believed that I had no hope of gaining Betty's forgiveness. August was always there and tried her best to reach out to me.

I betrayed both girls.

August and Betty don't deserve me right?

I do feel bad. I never wanted to be in a situation like this. The fog started to fill the air. The water kept falling down on my hood lightly. I was getting wetter.

I was praying that Dylan Blake or Ashton Gates would fuck off and not notice me here right now. I felt cold but at least I will be able to go to the tree with a swing.

She'll be there... Don't worry James. I shut my eyes trying to focus on walking and breathing. I still need to think of her.

Her red hair,
Her pinkish lips.
Her sad eyes.
And lonely bliss.

That was what I kept thinking. I have to be there in August. I have to stop loving Betty.

No more Betty and James. No more fun and games.

August and James can happen. And that was what I was thinking. August needs me now.

As I arrived home banging the door. I took a shower and changed my clothes as fast as I possibly could. My body was shaking from the cold. I tried my best to not lose balance by looking out of my bedroom window. There she was on the swing. The rain stopped.

I knew she arrived. Her Red hair was blown by the wind. It was dancing like flowers on a spring afternoon.

"August."

That's all I could say. I ran out of my house. Dad asked me why I'm leaving. I just kept quiet. He tried to stop me but I was like a lost puppy that finally found its rightful owner.

"James!" She cried out. Her eyes were happy that I finally didn't break my promise. This time at this place just to meet her by the swing.

"I told you I'll meet you here. Good thing you didn't get wet by the rain earlier."

I spread out my arms, wanting her to be embraced in a hug. Her arms folded and close to her chest. She was crying.

"What's wrong?" I asked her... I need to know the truth now. She should speak up or I might leave her here.

"I'm pregnant James! That's what is wrong. My mom disowned me after she saw my pregnancy kit. I don't kno-know what should do or how I re-really need to feel!"

I was speechless. The guess was right. The rumors about me and her turned out to be true. She did look like she gained weight in the past two months. It's confirmed...

And my teenage years came to an end.

In a blink of an eye, I'm going to her husband. I can't just leave August like this. Even if she didn't force me to marry her. I had to do so.

That's the right thing to do... Society shaping us teens into adulthood.

"August...Shhh. It's okay. I'll marry you. I don't care about what others say. We both know Betty had my heart. Now she must pass it to you."

August lifted her head to look into my eyes. Her eyes were still stuffed with tears. I can't help but watch her cry.

"James? You don't even love me at all. You told me in the locker room that you don't. Stop playing pretend! Stop lying!"
She demanded she try to push me away from her.

"I'm not. I just thought... You need me more today. If you do this alone. Raise up a child with no money. How will you and my unborn child survive?"

All the sweet days with Betty were now leaving my mind. I have to be a better person for August.

August and James don't sound right. But I'll make it right. Maybe this is what everyone wanted. Me and August to settle things together.

At least the illicit affairs with her would continue. Somehow, I'll learn to love August more.

Hoax

Betty's Point of view

"Dylan!!" As I screamed his name. It all started to blackout in an instant. Dylan started a fight earlier with James Robison, my ex-boyfriend. His punches on my ex made me feel empty. Why would they ever fight just to get me? I don't want to see this. I tried to stop him with all my might. I felt within me, A flame slowly dying. After accidentally getting hit by Dylan. I woke up here in the local hospital. Dylan was holding my hand. I searched for James and asked if he was also there. Then my mother told me that James was never allowed to visit me. Even my parents banned him from entering my room.

"What happened?" My thoughts were mixed up. I don't remember what happened to James. Did Dylan almost kill him? I just don't know... I'm already 18... Legal enough to have my own voice and mind. I didn't fight for James, nor did I ever wish to hate him. Moments that he was with me since I was 16. As an 18-year-old, this was my year of uncertainty.

Sadness filled the air, Dylan was there. His eyes look into mine. He was shaking like a nervous puppy in front of me. "Dylan...What happened to James?"

Dylan then turned cold. He froze at me mentioning James' name.

"He's fine. Don't worry about it, Betty."

For a second thought, was he lying? Was he really explaining to me the truth? All I remember was James sitting on the ground trying his best not to fight back. Dylan punched him with his fist going bloody. It wasn't what I expected to happen. A week later, I was able to manage to attend classes.

James was kneeling down in front of August. I was right to break up with him. I witnessed his marriage proposal for August. Dylan wasn't lying at all. James is alright with a smile on his face. I kind of felt the shivers in my body. The urge to puke was what I felt. This was outright disgusting for me to see.

Marriage? To James? Why would August have the audacity to marry such a douchebag! She doesn't deserve James... Neither did I deserve him.

James and August... That sounded pretty awful since I was part of that love triangle. Now I'm out of the picture, they are getting married.

Did I ever make a mistake? Why am I feeling so sad to see them kissing in front of me? The flashback of him. His lips on mine, his smell, everything. All of it was gone because of his affair with August. Did he ever think of me when he betrayed me?

The flashbacks... My memories of him got disintegrated. The polaroids he made for the both of us. Those pictures deserved burning. I never burnt it... I only placed it in the attic. Never returning the stuff he gave me. Even the cardigan he bought for me.

When classes ended. I hid in the art room. Crying by myself, after all... I don't deserve to be sad. Dylan knocked on the door of my art room.

"Betty Freeman." He called my name in frustration since the door was locked. "Why do you care so much, Dylan?" I asked still not opening the lock. "Betty! I've been for you all this time. Why wouldn't I care?" He did have a point... But this conversation feels pointless. Dylan and I should only remain best friends. Why would he want more of me? He even harmed me because of his jealousy of James.

"Leave me alone, I don't want you here!" He stood there I could see the lower part of his shoes under the door. I was sitting on the floor, knees closer to my chest. I could feel my heart sinking. My eyes were watery as tears continued streaming down my face. I didn't wipe my face with anything. I stayed silent, waiting for Dylan to leave.

"Betty, I know you still loved him. I just want him to stop hurting you anymore. He did it again. That fool! He only cares for himself and not you. He deceived you." Dylan's reasoning sounded deafening. A hex that made me under a spell to let him in my life again.

"Fine. I'll open the door. Just don't go too close to me." I wiped away my tears. The scars that James left upon me... The memories.

"Forget it, Betty, he has August now." My conscience told me. Despite all the hurt James caused months ago... I still haven't moved on as fast as he did. I unlocked the door letting Dylan come in. Dylan hugged me as fast as I opened the door.

"I told you I don't want you to be so close," I said as he pulled himself away. I was looking down at the floor. I know Dylan, he's been my best friend since grade school and became a new student here so that he could stay with me. He is loyal but clingy... This moment made me feel stronger. After the hoax that James did. After the months I've grown closer to Dylan.

"I want to shoot him dead. I just can't stop noticing him flaunt his new girl. Is he really serious about marrying her? I don't really care about Betty. As long as he is nowhere near you."

James and Betty were never meant to be I guess. I and James disconnected and grew farther away. After Senior year, he'll marry a girl named August Summers. It doesn't make any sense anymore. Part of me still loved him and part of me will never forgive him for what he did.

Dylan was always here for me, not James. Not like those silly puppies love he tricked me on. I only felt the burden James had become and not all those fun moments with him saying I love you...Kissing me on the porch of my house. Lying down under the stars while listening to music.

It didn't make any sense. Inez proved me wrong when she sent the photo. He could be a shitty person but he did make me smile before. But Dylan, he had been in my shadow. Constantly being there when I need my best bud the most.

I had chosen Dylan over James. It's my fault if I still love James. I'm totally fine now! Dylan Blake is mine... I am his, this can't change.

Dylan took my hand and asked me if I could go with him. To where? I didn't know.

All I know is that I trust Dylan now more than James. At least he won't hurt me again as he'd promised me. Protecting me at all costs. More than I can ever imagine being in love. The sense of trust was more important to me.

As I entered his car, he drove me to his home. Somewhere safer than the school. Somewhere I lost my thoughts of James. We didn't enter his bedroom. We just stayed in the living room and played games like the usual Dylan and Betty could. At that time, I enjoyed being with Dylan. I become freer on becoming myself. More of the colors turned bright and happy.

Finally, I could forget all about James and August.

In a place where everything becomes fixed like a painting made of little puzzle pieces.

Tears Ricochet

James' Point of view

Betty was there... In front of my classroom. I know I already proposed to August, but I can't help seeing her face. She knocked on the door hoping the teacher would let her in. Mr. Markus twisted the doorknob and opened it with a small gap. He asked her what she needed. Then she told him if he can excuse me to talk to her. Her eyes... I can't stop thinking about what I did wrong. She is the one who decided to break up with me. Her parents even banned me so I couldn't visit her in the hospital. Dylan was kinda dumb to knock her out accidentally. Many years of my time being with Betty had already ended.

All that time just got wasted...

Mr. Markus said that it was okay for her to talk to me since I completed my last submission of my homework.

"What is it now Betty?"

I don't know what to ask her. It is really confusing on which words won't hurt her the most. Yes, she was my first and only girlfriend. I lost her and it is me to blame. Years with her was the best experience I got.

But I know...She deserves better.

Someone better than me. I then sensed tears streaming down from my left eye. I felt horrible at this moment. *What kind of question was that, James?*

How should I act around her after what I did with August?

She then placed her hand beside my left cheek to wipe away the tears. My tears ricochet and made my hands tremble by stopping myself from removing her hand from my face. Nervous I was around this girl. August...What about August? I am already destined to marry her after graduation.

I can't imagine a life without this girl in front of me.

Betty...

Betty.

All my thoughts are filled with what-ifs. Is this the last time I will be able to see her?

Her touch,

her kiss...

Her embrace.

Her lovely grace...

Her masterpiece of artworks.

Her love that lasts forever?

None of that I deserve. None of it! She reminds me of how the fire kept me warm in the winter. Of how I died inside as she dumped me.

None of that matters now. I'll always remain as her past lover. My silence broke down as she heard my voice.

"I'm sorry about everything." She just smiled like an angel from heaven. Every passing moment was crucial for me to wait and hear her voice again.

"It's alright...Humans like us make mistakes. I hope you are feeling better now. I now know everything. I just got jealous of how you treat August like your Queen. Like she had always been better than me for you to love. I just got out of the hospital. I don't think I could fix things with Dylan. So...Now you got a new girlfriend. Take care of her, as you did to me when we were together."

"I know and it's time that we make amends and let go of each other... August is pregnant. And I can't change things because I cheated on you."

She then bursts into tears. I can't hug her like before. Staying away from her was what I can do to make no one notice how much I still love her.

Distance is what I needed.

After all the trouble I caused...

My classmates are watching me now.

That meant the whole school would know about this encounter.

"Stop crying, don't waste your tears for me. I never wanted to see you like this. Betty...Please stop crying in front of me."

I begged her... I need to end this conversation, it is going nowhere.

"I'm not okay James. You know how much everything had fallen into place. Dylan hates you. Ashton hates you... You guys fought and I just can't help seeing you almost getting murdered by them. It really sucks!"

She forced herself to smile. The empty halls made our voices echo louder than usual. The sadness I felt was nothing compared to hers. I wished I could tell her everything I felt... I can't anymore. Both of us have separate fates. Mine was intertwined with August while she was now with Dylan.

"I don't know how I can say farewell. Maybe Goodbye is better. I need to leave you here." Betty reminds me of the joy we once shared. She walked away and look back at me as she entered her classroom.

My fault for being drunk at prom night.

My fault for following August that night.

My fault for becoming jealous of Dylan and Betty.

She looks so happy with him.

I wasn't there because I was never like Dylan.

I was never her close childhood best friend.

Her blue eyes...Her blonde golden hair. Everything colorful about her turned my world into a darkness that I can't escape. My mouth was shut into a serious look I put on. August was inside my classroom and I think she heard me. Mr. Markus smiled at me for no proper reason. "Love problems right lover-boy?" Inez said and laughed as hard as she normally would. My other classmates laughed with her. I knew I was a jerk from that day. Inez then took a paper from her notebook and handed it over to August.

August opened it and then she covered her mouth when she saw what's in it.

"Ashton asked me to give that to you. Summer bummer. Hahaha!"

Inez laughed at her while August crumpled the paper and threw it at her forehead. "Gossip B*tch!" August covered her mouth and looked at Me. Markus who was still here in class. I picked up the crumpled paper and was about to open it. Mr. Markus asked me to hand the paper to him. I gave it to him.

"Inez, you and Ashton will be in detention. Miss Summers and Mr. Robinson, meet me at the faculty office later.

"Ughh, fine sir." Inez rolled her eyes and looked at Ashton who winked at her. She then smirked like a bully.

"Dear August. We know you are going to be a teenage pregnant queen. Congrats on being a whore who stole James from Betty. Sincerely, Ashton and Inez."

Mr. Markus paused and looked disappointed with how childish his senior high students were. "So, is this true James? I thought you were a responsible student. I need to report this to our principal."

Even though the marriage proposal was in secret. I never told the school about the mistake me and August made.

Waahhh!!!(Me screaming inside)
*What the hell should I do **now**?*

Mad Woman

August Summer's Point of view

After he asked to marry me near the swing. James has been constantly there for me and our baby. Since my parents disowned me, I've been living with James and his father.

Both of them are so kind and gentle. James sometimes looks sad. I remember how his hands held mine as we walk home that day he proposed to me. His hands filled with warmth and his fingers interlocked with mine.

He is beautiful.

Or I mean handsome, in many ways.

His flaws made me see how much he changed since the day I met him in the cafeteria.

How he would fight against the enemies of the people he loves. How his eyes sparkle when he looks at Betty instead of me. How his words may hurt but were the honest truth.

Inez and Ashton always got a chance to prank call or even annoy me. I kept telling them to get a life and stop spying on me.

Ashton was different from James. Ashton would often be a maniac and touch me everywhere when kissing me. He would be happy-go-lucky like a total corny clown. I hated him.

I hated him after he and Inez started gossiping around the school about me.

Most of the time I would end up in the library sleeping and the librarian would wake me up when the bell rang. Sometimes my parents would ask me to come back to them.

They just can't handle the fact that I'm going to be a mother sooner than them.

I'm already 18... And they still treat me like a child. If only the world would stop revolving around my own mistakes. Perhaps if I talk to Betty.

While in class. I watched James approach Betty. He wasn't looking alright. His watery eyes forced him not to cry.

She was there...
His first love.
His first kiss.
She should be mad at me, not him...

I heard their conversation. When James went back into the classroom. He looked at me then looked at Inez. Inez talked to James... She handed me a paper written in Ashton's handwriting. As I read this I almost had the urge to cry. I crumpled the paper as hard as I can and threw it at her. "Gossip Bitch!" I shouted at her. James picked up the paper and almost read it until Mr. Markus got it from him.

"Fuck." I whispered to myself and James didn't hear me curse.

After class... Mr. Markus made me remove my jacket to see the bump on my belly. "Mr. Robinson and Ms. Summers, what really happened a few months ago? We conducted an investigation into this case. You know that this school tries its best to avoid teenage pregnancies. It is your responsibility after you graduate to marry her. You might lose the chance to get a scholarship after this incident. Please explain to us why Betty Freeman ended up in a hospital. *How August got pregnant because of you and how Inez is responsible for the rumors spreading."*

James stuttered before he spoke clearly. "It's my fault sir. I and August got drunk after prom night. I and Betty broke up and her relationship with Dylan blossomed. Inez was spying on me and August while telling everyone on social media. Dylan, Ashton, and I got into a fight. Dylan knocked her out by accident. I never intend to fight them... I was protecting myself. I ignored August for weeks or maybe a few months. Then a week earlier I found out she got pregnant. It's my fault sir."

"I got a call from August Summers' parents. Mr. and Mrs. Summer told me that you can't marry their daughter."

James looked at me... He was lost for words. My parents... Why the hell they won't give me the chance to be happy for once?

"James, you should meet her parents before marrying her. You are both too young to become parents. Please abide by the rules of the school."

James put his arms around me. I could feel his heart beating fast. I didn't know what to do. I just stood there and did not mind hugging him back.

"The principal and guidance counselor will be here soon. Please wait for them."

The door creaked open. Betty was the first to enter the room. Followed by the principal named Mrs. Farvald and Mr. Andrew the guidance counselor and the class adviser.

"Why is she here?" James asked in a low tone of surprise. Mrs. Farvald is an elderly widowed woman who rarely is seen around campus because she always stays in her office doing files and records of students. She sometimes calls students in her office when it comes to detentions and warnings. Her platinum blonde hair and green eyes are pleasing enough to make you feel welcome in school. Now she wears a frown and her old rose formal attire shows how she fulfills her responsibilities around this campus.

"Betty is a witness. Both of you know that it is forbidden for students to be pregnant before they even graduate senior high school."

"I and August are going to be expelled?" James was wide-eyed and in shock about what was happening right now.

"No, August won't be allowed to attend college until she gives birth to your child. It is certain Mr. Robison will be under observation because Ms. Summer's parents requested to see if he would be good for their only daughter."

James then turned to look at Betty. Betty didn't smile or frown. She brought herself up to look serious with pride and dignity.

"Ms. Freeman, tell us what you think about this situation?"

"I feel like I am a mad woman who is angry about what my ex-boyfriend did. But I forgave him. He doesn't need to be in observation. He is a rightful person to marry August. Everything happened by accident."

Betty then smiled for once. I try to get my jacket back on so that they won't notice the baby bump anymore.

At the end of this month, Mr. Markus, Mr. Andrews, and Mrs. Farvald decided to do what Mr. Markus's punishment was.

Inez got a week's suspension along with her boyfriend. All of us graduated with flying colors.

The Last American Dynasty

"Mark my words... I love you August. And will continue to do so forever." James kissed her passionately. August had already given birth and named their daughter Rebekah Robison. August's mother carried the baby during the wedding. She was so pleased that James was a good fit for her only daughter.

August's red hair was like a flame that flowed like a river and was now curled into a bun. Flowers perched on her hair. The wedding was near August's father-in-law's house.

It was simple yet elegant. The red roses formed an arch and the guest was seated on church benches that have a gap in the blue carpet on the grassy ground.

Betty was there. She was invited to attend this wedding. If only James called her name, she would be his bride-to-be instead of August. Time was cruel enough for her. Dylan sat beside her, in all that angst and anger against James, he got a soft heart for Betty.

The wedding bells rang. As they watch August in the back part of the guest. Everyone was shocked at how beautiful she was on that day.

It's hard to describe a beautiful woman without seeing the flaws on their face. But because of those flaws, it got covered in makeup, enhancing her beauty like a Queen ready to marry her King.

James went out of his house and ran towards the pastor. He stood there like a statue, nervously clenching his fist at the sight of his ex-girlfriend and her new boyfriend.

His focus turned to August. He realizes how much of lucky a person he had become. How August was smiling like a fairy that gracefully walks towards him.

All he could do was smile. He also turned his gaze onto his firstborn Daughter. Such a lovely couple they are. If only there was a way he could forget Betty completely, he would. Despite thinking of her, he made Betty his daughter's godmother.

The delight in his eyes to see August in her beautiful white cocktail dress that had a train of white laced cloth that flowed when the wind softly blew it up. Two flower girls then grab a hold of the train of lace. All of them walking on the aile's red carpet. The two bridesmaids, Katie Denver and Marzie Baker followed the bride-to-be.

James smiled in his blue tuxedo and black ribbon. It was a beautiful wedding. It's enough for James and August to manage. James starts to have feelings for August. He is no longer obsessed with Betty.

The pastor began to speak until he ask the bride and the groom if they will agree to their matrimony. They both said yes and the pastor smiled before saying: "You may kiss the bride."

---

14 years later:

On a winter morning. James, August, and their daughter lived together in St. Louis.

"Mother, I wanted to tell you something!" Her daughter, Rebekah said with excitement.

"Yes, darling what is it?" August placed her daughter's hair behind her ear. "I have a new boyfriend!"

"Mind if you tell me?" Rebekah nodded. She was abundant with joy. A bubbly and happy teenage girl. James entered the room. "What are you two girls up to this time?"

"Mom and I are talking about my new boyfriend." Rebekah grinned at her own remark.

"Who is it, sweetie?" James asked then August giggled. "His name is Bill."

"He sounds rich," James replied he then carried his daughter to her bedroom.

"I'll put her to sleep. Happy Mother's Day August." James said and closed the door with his left hand.

"Thanks." August smiled and went back to sleep on her queen-sized bed.

James worked so hard to provide for their family. August got her college education when James had enough for August to achieve her dreams. It all had fallen into place.

A decade later,

Rebekah was riding on an afternoon train, she was a twenty-four-year-old woman who married Bill who is the owner of a famous standard oil company. But she already divorced him and signed the papers. He received it and his heart gave out. Which made her control his assets while he was at the hospital.

She thought of her family back in St. Louis. But the sunshine removes her mind from the past. Her parents would enjoy their time with her. She always knew that her father loved someone else. She just didn't know who it is. She entered her beach box house alone. Nobody else was there.

Their wedding was charming. But the parties weren't as fun as her neighbors. It lacked the loud noises and the fun. It was difficult for her to be seen as a divorcée. Her former father in law named Dylan Blake was telling her about how he met James Robison, her father. She never believed that her father was like that before.

She didn't care anymore. Dylan is her close neighbor that owns a chihuahua. Dylan Blake was the reason why she can't stand being with her ex-husband.

Rebekah stole her father-in-law's dog. She placed the chihuahua in her bathtub. She poured the key lime green dye and started to wash the female chihuahua with her shampoo for it to stay that color. She cried by herself with laughter just like a mad... crazy woman herself.

She gave back the dog the next day. Rebekah enjoyed parties with the big names in the Hollywood industry.

She even made scripts for movies that connect with her in her own life.

She was happy.
All by herself.
No man to take care of.
Only herself.

The last person in her family, no kids, a dying husband...Just a rotting dynasty left to her.

The Last American Dynasty!

They said she was seen occasionally pacing rocks and throwing them into the midnight sea.

She had a marvelous time ruining the things around her. Holiday house sat quietly on the beach. Undisturbed for 50 years... Rebekah gave up her beach house and Taylor Swift bought her Rhode Island house.

Rebekah then went on back to her parent's house. Her parents lived together forever.

And she never heard about her father's ex-girlfriend named Betty.

In Jame's last moments,

He called for Betty. Something that never happened again.

Betty was long gone.

So Betty and James didn't exist anymore.

Exile

"I hate the ending."

Betty ran towards James. She hugged him tight and never wanted to let go like before. August was in India for a business trip. His daughter was away and married to Bill. It was 24 years. 24 years apart from each other.

"I missed you," Betty said with happiness in her voice. "Perhaps we both hate how this ended." James then noticed the wrinkles on her face. His gaze and sweet disposition made Betty happy again.

"Probably... I've been in love with you since we were 16. But after all that had happened. I forgot what you did with August. You know I'm sick right now and can die any moment soon."

James Robison,
and
Betty Freeman.

Two lovers who had been cursed by reality. Of how things turned out to be the worst. How Dylan and Betty's wedding never happened. Dylan married some other girl named Natasha. Then had a son named Bill Blake. Bill inherited a huge amount of riches. Then he married James' daughter and got a divorce few years later. And now Betty and James finally reunited.

Both of them are bidding their farewells after years apart.

"I got the cardigan you gave me when we were seventeen." James hugged her and then kissed her forehead.

"We'll still remain good friends and that is important to me." Betty then kissed James' cheek. It made him blush.

"Let's watch a free movie together?" James asked. Betty nodded in agreement.

"How about La-la-land?" Betty asked him, this movie personally resonated with her.

"I've seen that before and didn't like the ending." They went inside the mall and watched together. Betty fell asleep on his shoulder. He didn't realize she wasn't breathing anymore. That she aged like fine wine but got spilled far from his fingertips. The movie they watched also had a tragic ending.

Betty didn't get to see it.

She's sick enough to fade away.

She died silently on his right shoulder. James cried and calling out her name was his very last word.

©Exile by Taylor Swift:

can see you standin', honey
With his arms around your body

*Laughin' but the joke's not funny at all
And it took you five whole minutes
To pack us up and leave me with it
Holdin' all this love out here in the hall
I think I've seen this film before
And I didn't like the ending
You're not my homeland anymore
So what am I defendin' now?
You were my town
Now I'm in exile seein' you out
I think I've seen this film before
Hoo, hoo-ooh
Hoo, hoo-ooh
Hoo, hoo-ooh
I can see you starin', honey
Like he's just your understudy
Like you'd get your knuckles bloody for me
Second, third, and hundredth chances
Balancin' on breaking branches
Those eyes add insult to injury
I think I've seen this film before
And I didn't like the ending
I'm not your problem anymore
So who am I offending now?
You were my crown
Now I'm in exile seein' you out
I think I've seen this film before
So I'm leavin' out the side door
So step right out
There is no amount
Of cryin', I can do for you*

All this time
We always walked a very thin line
You didn't even hear me out (you didn't even
hear me out)
You never gave a warning sign (I gave so many
signs)
All this time
I never learned to read your mind (never learned
to read my mind)
I couldn't turn things around (you never turned
things around)
'Cause you never gave a warning sign (I gave so
many signs)
So many signs
So many signs (you didn't even see the signs)
I think I've seen this film before
And I didn't like the ending
You're not my homeland anymore
So what am I defending now?
You were my town
Now I'm in exile seein' you out
I think I've seen this film before
So I'm leaving out the side door
So step right out
There is no amount
Of cryin', I can do for you
All this time
We always walked a very thin line
You didn't even hear me out (you didn't even
hear me out)
You never gave a warning sign (I gave so many

signs)
All this time
I never learned to read your mind (never learned to read my mind)
I couldn't turn things around (you never turned things around)
'Cause you never gave a warning sign (I gave so many signs)
All this time (so many signs)
I never learned to read your mind (so many signs)
I couldn't turn things around (so many signs)
'Cause you never gave a warning sign (never gave a warning sign)

The song played as an ending. James brought Betty to the hospital. It was all too late. He will miss her no matter what.

He never told his wife and daughter about his love for Betty Freeman.
About how he was exiled by society after his scandalous affair with August.

- - - - - - - -

Life just happens so unexpectedly. You won't even realize the impact you give on others' lives. Betty and James did happen in the past. Until the tables turned until the glass dropped onto the ground.

Death will take people you love.
You will stand the test of time just like James.

You will give a chance to forgive those who wronged you like Betty.
You will find someone who'll accept you like August.

Remember, you aren't alone in this world. You can have friends or none. It's up to you and it is your choice whether you like folklore by Taylor Swift or not.

Love develops pain.
Pain within love triangles.
Pain within society shapes our beliefs.

People tend to forget the little things around us. This story... Will forever remain as a memory. A memory shared by your favorite singer, Taylor Swift.

- - - - -

James Robison then moved on with his life. He even tried his best to never forget.
All the people in his life come and go.

Especially, Betty,
he will never forget about her.
And this is where his story ends.

This is where his relationship with Betty was kept a secret from his daughter. And in his last words, he would call out her name.

"Betty..." And in the whip of his air and soul floating away from his body. Betty met him there and they both walked their way to a path called the bridge of life and *death*.

Peace

"*James?*" *August opened the door. She then approached James on his bed. His eyes looked sad. He pressed his fingers on the bed sheet. Closing his eyes as August kissed his cheek.*

"What happened, is everything alright?" James shrugged his shoulders. He wasn't smiling when he saw August like he always had.

"No, I'm not! It's Betty who died earlier."

"I knew you would meet each other *again*." August fought herself from crying. All these years? It was hard for her to be a mother to her only daughter. They grew older and time made her feel an ache in her. It was like when the hard rain crashed down hard.

"I moved on and seeing her gave me peace. I know you aren't happy about it August." He then took the cardigan and passed it on to her.

"That was the last gift I gave her years ago. Before you met me. It kills me deeply when I remember what happened." James sighed. He hugged August. He aged like fine wine. He became a better person when he met August. Marrying August was the best decision he ever made.

"This was her favorite cardigan... She wore it happily until her *last hour.*"

"You changed me, James. I'm so sorry for ruining your relationship with her. I'm afraid we can't turn back time." August leaned down her head onto Jame's shoulder.

"Don't blame yourself August! You are an amazing wife and a beautiful mother." James turned his body towards August and kissed her. His eyes looked at her like he always did.

He finally had a sense of <u>peace</u> in his heart and let go of his past with Betty.

About the Author

Kathryn_Folklore

Katherine enjoys reading stories, writing, drawing and expressing herself through art.

Her favorite books are by Chris Colfer. She enjoys music by Taylor Swift and Olivia Rodrigo. She is also a dreamer; she tends to imagine her life like she's living in a dream. Some People in her Life supports her in her dream. This inspires her more to achieve her goals. She fell in love with writing this story and hope she can Touch the lives of others by writing this novella's short story.

She is now enjoying her college life, making new friends, and exploring the aspects of her life to the fullest (2022). She is the author of the poetry collection titled: "Heart and Holes of Void.

www.ingramcontent.com/pod-product-compliance
Lightning Source LLC
LaVergne TN
LVHW041623070526
838199LV00052B/3217